MOLLY PITCHER

Kathleen E. Bradley

Assistant Editor
Leslie Huber, M.A.

Editorial Director
Dona Herweck Rice

Editor-in-Chief
Sharon Coan, M.S.Ed.

Editorial Manager
Gisela Lee, M.A.

Creative Director
Lee Aucoin

Illustration Manager/Designer
Timothy J. Bradley

Cover Art and Illustration
Chad Thompson

Publisher
Rachelle Cracchiolo, M.S.Ed.

Teacher Created Materials, Inc.
5301 Oceanus Drive
Huntington Beach, CA 92649-1030
http://www.tcmpub.com
ISBN 978-1-4333-0993-9
©2010 Teacher Created Materials, Inc.

Molly Pitcher

Story Summary

The battles of the Revolutionary War are being fought, and every Patriot is needed. Molly Hays follows her husband William to war to do what she can to help. She cooks and sews for the army. When the men suffer from the heat, she carries them water in a pitcher. The water is also used to cool the cannons of battle. This is how she earns her name, Molly Pitcher.

While Molly works, she performs amazing feats. She feeds thousands at once. She gives water to dozens from the same pitcher—at the same time. She even straightens a river to make the water run faster!

When Molly's husband is wounded in battle, the courageous woman takes up his cannon. General Washington sees her heroism and names her a sergeant among his army of only men. Molly Pitcher becomes a true American hero!

Tips for Performing Reader's Theater

Adapted from Aaron Shepard

- Don't let your script hide your face. If you can't see the audience, your script is too high.

- Look up often when you speak. Don't just look at your script.

- Talk slowly so the audience knows what you are saying.

- Talk loudly so everyone can hear you.

- Talk with feelings. If the character is sad, let your voice be sad. If the character is surprised, let your voice be surprised.

- Stand up straight. Keep your hands and feet still.

- Remember that even when you are not talking, you are still your character.

- Narrator, be sure to give the characters enough time for their lines.

Tips for Performing
Reader's Theater *(cont.)*

- If the audience laughs, wait for them to stop before you speak again.

- If someone in the audience talks, don't pay attention.

- If someone walks into the room, don't pay attention.

- If you make a mistake, pretend it was right.

- If you drop something, try to leave it where it is until the audience is looking somewhere else.

- If a reader forgets to read his or her part, see if you can read the part instead, make something up, or just skip over it. Don't whisper to the reader!

- If a reader falls down during the performance, pretend it didn't happen.

Molly Pitcher

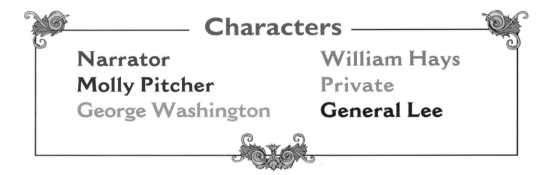

Characters

Narrator	William Hays
Molly Pitcher	Private
George Washington	**General Lee**

Setting

This reader's theater takes place during the Revolutionary War. The action peaks at the battle of Monmouth in New Jersey in June 1778.

Act 1

Narrator:	It is June 18, 1778, and America is at war with England.
Private:	General Washington, the redcoats are marching to New York!
Washington:	We must stop them. Private, gather my generals.
Private:	Yes, sir!
Narrator:	A meeting is held at Valley Forge to discuss battle plans. Major General Charles Lee, Washington's senior officer, is quick to voice his doubts about a full attack.
General Lee:	General Washington, our troops lack the skills to fight the world's finest army.
Washington:	Our army has received special training.
General Lee:	The British have more troops. They were well cared for this past winter. Your troops barely survived the cold, hunger, and disease that were here.
Washington:	You don't know my soldiers' hardships!

General Lee: I know that a full attack is unwise at this point. We should send small parties to sabotage the British.

Washington: I do not agree. We will pursue the army and engage them in a full attack. Gather your men and prepare to depart!

General Lee: Yes, sir.

Narrator: Across the field, Molly Hays sits under a tree. Her white ruffled cap is pushed back on her head. She sews a soldier's shirt. Her husband, William, sits nearby.

William Hays: Molly, we have received orders to move out of Valley Forge today.

Narrator: Molly looks up. She spits the needle that is in her mouth squarely into her pincushion. Then she thrusts the cushion into her pocket like a soldier returning his sword to its case.

Molly Pitcher: Leaving? When I still have a hundred uniforms to sew?

William Hays: Those are the orders. No use complaining, soldier.

Molly Pitcher: All right then, let me feed your empty stomachs. Listen for the bell.

Narrator: Molly travels with the army. She sews and cooks for the soldiers. She prepares breakfast and rings the bell.

Private: Last one in line goes without breakfast!

Molly Pitcher: Okay, boys, line up. Shoulders back. Dishes faceup!

William Hays: Yes, ma'am!

Molly Pitcher: I will not have my firecakes and eggs dropped on this muddy field.

William Hays: Yes, but ... firecakes? Molly, why did you go and bake those? Once Congress sent us food, I thought we'd never be forced to eat them again!

Private: I agree! They're awful.

Narrator: Molly has a glint in her eye as she wipes her arm across her forehead.

Molly Pitcher: Awful, eh? Do my ears deceive me?

Private:	Pardon me, ma'am. All the firecakes that I have eaten were as hard as musket balls and . . .
William Hays:	Watch your step, son, and tread lightly.
Narrator:	Molly grabs one of her firecake biscuits. She pretends to wind up for a fierce pitch at the young private.
William Hays:	The young man was just stating his opinion. Isn't that one of the reasons we're fighting this war?
Molly Pitcher:	Rightly so, William. Thankfully, I am feeling patriotic this morning, so I will spare the boy. All right then, who's hungry?
William Hays:	We all are!
Molly Pitcher:	Very well, man your plates.
Narrator:	Then, with the agility of a circus performer, Molly grabs dozens of eggs from the basket beside her. With her left hand, she tosses them into the air, one by one, juggling them in a circle above her head. As each egg falls into her right hand, she cracks it before it lands perfectly into the hot frying pan.

William Hays: Molly, these are the finest scrambled eggs ever.

Molly Pitcher: Of course! My juggling scrambles them before the yolks hit the pan!

Narrator: The Continental army packs up and moves out. General Washington meets with his officers.

Washington: Gentlemen, General Lee will attack the rear flank of the British army. An equal army of men will circle around and attack the front.

General Lee: The British have more troops! I warn you, this strategy is sure to fail.

Washington: The spirit of this army cannot fail.

General Lee: No amount of spirit will make up for the lack of soldiers.

Washington: There is nothing worse than a commander unsure about his troops. General Lafayette, will you lead the attack?

General Lee: Step back, Lafayette. You're nothing but a boy. I won't give up this mission to a lesser man.

Washington: Very well, General Lee. Plan your attack.

Act 2

Narrator: On the morning of June 28, 1778, the sun rises quickly—two whole hours before dawn! It sends strong rays of light across the land, scorching all in its path. Every living thing thirsts for water that day. Continental soldiers line up and advance on the British army.

General Lee: Officers, stand ready for my orders. I will send them to the battlefield.

Molly Pitcher: Now, William, do not get riled. General Lee must know what he's doing.

William Hays: A commander should not withhold orders before battle. How will we know what to do?

Molly Pitcher: All you need to do is point your cannon and fire on those Redcoats.

General Lee: Fire!

Narrator: Musket shots ring out from both sides. William Hays, the first gunner of his cannon team, rams and sponges the cannon muzzle.

William Hays: Swabbing! Molly, get water. This sponge is dry!

Narrator:	William takes the long wooden pole with a rag at one end and jams it into the cannon. Molly brings water to cool the cannon. Lee inspects the men.
General Lee:	Faster, soldiers! Ready, aim, fire!
William Hays:	Yes, sir! Molly, we need your pitcher! Where is she?
Private:	Running back toward the stream to fetch more cool water.
William Hays:	Very well. Stand back! Swabbing!
Private:	Cartridge! Fire!
William Hays:	Whew! We need Molly right away. We can't have even a hint of flame from the last shot, or this cannon will explode. Molly, where are you?
Molly Pitcher:	I am right here, William, with water for the sponge.
William Hays:	Fine work. Private, load the cartridge again!
Private:	Yes, sir. I have a full sack of black powder.
Molly Pitcher:	Look out!

Narrator: A cannon ball lands behind them, striking four soldiers. They fall to the ground, and Molly rushes to their side. Three are dead, but one cries out.

Molly Pitcher: Don't you worry, lad. I'll take care of you.

Narrator: Molly, although small, has the strength of a team of draft horses. In one swift, sure move, she tosses the soldier over her shoulder and carries him to safety.

Molly Pitcher: Soldier, let me dress that wound and then I'll fetch you some water. But look at this. The stream isn't running fast enough to quench the thirst of twelve thousand men and swab the cannons. This won't do.

Narrator: With both feet firmly planted, Molly straddles the streambed. She bends over it and drives her arms beneath the rich soil. With one great tug, she jerks the streambed and straightens it out flat and wide.

Molly Pitcher: There you go! That's more like it.

Private: Molly, pitcher!

Molly Pitcher: Coming! There must be a better way to quench the thirst of these brave patriots.

Narrator: The sounds of battle are everywhere. Molly's name is called again and again. She runs in every direction, helping each soldier in turn. Then she gets an idea. She holds her pitcher in the line of fire. Several musket balls strike the pitcher, and water spurts everywhere. Molly showers dozens of soldiers with drinking water at once.

Act 3

Narrator: By afternoon, the battle spreads. The weather grows hotter. Molly looks around and sees hundreds of men fainting from the heat.

Molly Pitcher: General Lee is handing out orders. Why can't he order up some rain?

General Lee: Men, fall back and reload. Fall back!

Narrator: The first line of soldiers obeys Lee's command. They move with such haste that the other men believe they have been ordered to retreat.

William Hays: Pull back? Nonsense. We have held our ground all day.

Narrator:	Confusion follows as hundreds of men run from the battlefield. General Washington, hearing of the panic, sends a message to General Lee.
Washington:	General Lee, send me the details of the battle.
Private:	General Washington, there's mass disorder. General Lee does not respond.
Washington:	Take me to him now.
Narrator:	Washington charges toward the front line. He meets retreating soldiers.
Washington:	Where is your officer? What are your orders?
Narrator:	The exhausted soldiers say they have been given no orders. They have simply pointed their guns and fired. Their officer is missing. Then, Washington spies Lee.
Washington:	General Lee, what is the reason for this disorder? Why did you order a retreat?
General Lee:	I did not order a retreat. I ordered one unit to fall back. Others followed.

Washington: This happened because you did not form a plan for your officers.

General Lee: The men ran in every direction. I told you they are not fit to fight.

Washington: Sir, your duty is to direct your soldiers. You'll be dealt with later.

Private: Not all the troops have run, sir. There's a cannon line holding firm.

Washington: Private, take me to that line!

Narrator: Washington rallies the men, and they charge forward to strike the British.

Act 4

Narrator: Molly dashes from the stream to the cannons, her pitcher sloshing with water. Upon returning to her husband's cannon, she sees him fall to the ground.

Molly Pitcher: William! Are you hurt?

Narrator:	William, dazed and sick, cannot respond. He is weak from heat exposure. The team leader, seeing William down, orders his team back.
Molly Pitcher:	William, get up! Your team needs you.
Narrator:	Molly looks around at the crew. They are weak from the heat. She grabs the swabber and thrusts the wooden pole into the muzzle of the cannon.
Molly Pitcher:	There's no need to fall back, sir. I'm taking William's place!
Narrator:	Molly looks into the eyes of the men. Her energy inspires them. The commander shouts, "What are you waiting for? Listen to her!"
Molly Pitcher:	Swab! Load the cartridge, Private! Ram! Fire!
Narrator:	With each fire, Molly calls out a reason for the fight against the British.
Molly Pitcher:	Take this one for threatening our freedom! And another for burning our homes! Here's one for the harsh taxes!

Narrator:	As the sun sets, General Washington rides his horse alongside the cannon line. Through the smoke, he sees the form of a young woman beside a cannon.
Private:	Molly! We're out of cannon shot.
Molly Pitcher:	Let me see what's in my apron pockets. Yes, this firecake and pincushion will do. Swab! Load! Ram! Fire! Take that back to your greedy English king!
Narrator:	Thirteen metal pins shoot out of the cannon, piercing the night air. The heat of the exploding gunpowder mixed with a large dose of patriotism causes an aurora of red, white, and blue that stretches across the skies. Thirteen white stars form a perfect circle on the star-spangled banner in the sky. When the British see this sight, they drop their rifles and flee the battlefield. The battle is over. Molly kneels at her husband's side.

Song: The Star-Spangled Banner

William Hays:	Oh, Molly, what did you just do?
Molly Pitcher:	Just my fair share, nothing more.

Act 5

Private:	Molly, General Washington sent me to find you.
Molly Pitcher:	Me? Are you sure?
Private:	I'm certain of it. He saw you with the cannon.
Narrator:	Molly wipes her hands on her apron and straightens her cap on her head.
Molly Pitcher:	Do I look all right, William? Am I fit to meet the general?
William Hays:	You are the best-looking soldier in this army!
Private:	If you'd like, we'll all come with you, Molly. We'll be sure he knows that we couldn't have held the cannon without you.
Narrator:	Molly and the entire army of soldiers stride across the camp to Washington's tent. The general steps outside. He towers over Molly. The army of soldiers surrounds her. Washington grins at the sight. Molly curtsies.

Molly Pitcher: General Washington, I am Molly Hays. It is an honor to meet you.

Washington: Mrs. Hays, I was moved by your courage on the battlefield.

Molly Pitcher: Why, I was simply doing my part.

Washington: You are too modest. If not for you, a cannon would have been pulled from battle. Every cannon fired is fired for freedom. For your efforts, I give you the title of Sergeant in our Continental army. You have served your country well.

Narrator: The men cheer loudly, and Molly laughs heartily.

William Hays: Molly, must we salute you now?

Molly Pitcher: That's Sergeant Molly, Private, and don't you forget it!

Narrator: Then the Patriots of Washington's army raise Molly onto their shoulders. They dance through the streets, shouting, "Three cheers for Sergeant Molly!"

Poem: Molly Pitcher

Molly Pitcher

by Kate Brownlee Sherwood

It was hurry and scurry at Monmouth town,
For Lee was beating a wild retreat;
The British were riding the Yankee down,
And panic was pressing on flying feet.

Galloping down like a hurricane
Washington rode with his sword swung high,
Mighty as he of the Trojan plain
Fired by a courage from the sky.

"Halt, and stand to your guns!" he cried.
And a bombardier made swift reply.
Wheeling his cannon into the tide,
He fell 'neath the shot of a foeman high.

Molly Pitcher sprang to his side,
Fired as she saw her husband do.
Telling the king in his stubborn pride
Women like men to their homes are true.

Washington rode from the bloody fray
Up to the gun that a woman manned.
"Molly Pitcher, you saved the day,"
He said, as he gave her a hero's hand.

He named her sergeant with manly praise,
While her war-brown face was wet with tears—
A woman has ever a woman's ways,
And the army was wild with cheers.

The Star-Spangled Banner

by Francis Scott Key

Oh, say can you see by the dawn's early light
What so proudly we hailed at the twilight's last gleaming?
Whose broad stripes and bright stars through the perilous fight,
O'er the ramparts we watched were so gallantly streaming?
And the rocket's red glare, the bombs bursting in air,
Gave proof through the night that our flag was still there.
Oh, say does that star-spangled banner yet wave
O'er the land of the free and the home of the brave?

On the shore, dimly seen through the mists of the deep,
Where the foe's haughty host in dread silence reposes,
What is that which the breeze, o'er the towering steep,
As it fitfully blows, half conceals, half discloses?
Now it catches the gleam of the morning's first beam,
In full glory reflected now shines in the stream:
'Tis the star-spangled banner! Oh, long may it wave
O'er the land of the free and the home of the brave!

Glossary

aurora—a natural phenomenon where brightly colored lights streak across the night sky; typically seen in the skies close to the magnetic poles

bombardier—a member of a bombing crew

commander—an officer of high rank in the service, in charge of a unit of men

firecake—a hard biscuit made of flour and water made for the troops during the Revolutionary War

flank—the extreme right or left side of an army or fleet

patriot—a person who is dedicated to his or her country and is willing to protect it at all costs

perilous—dangerous

pincushion—a soft ball of cloth that pins are stuck into for safe storage

ramparts—the protected upper parts of a fortress

retreat—to pull back from enemy forces to seek safety